MESSENGER OF *Christ*

DANIEL JEAN-LOUIS

ISBN   Softcover   978-1-950596-79-9
            Ebook   978-1-948801-82-9

Printed in the United States of America.

BookWhip
1545 S. Harbor Blvd., #2001,
Fullerton, CA 92832

DEDICATION

I dedicate this book to my dad, Elius Jean-Louis.
Thank you for being there for me.

ACKNOWLEDGEMENTS

Thank you to my good friend Loleta Washington, who was the only person that believed in what I was doing.

Special thanks to Matt Amsden, Shai Wilson, and Michael Gier of Silver Dove Productions.

NOTE FROM THE AUTHOR

Before you begin reading *Messenger of Christ*, please visit messengerofchrist.world and watch the video there.

Once you reach Chapter Eight in the book where Chelsea is singing Elton John's "Daniel", stop reading and listen to that song. Therein, you will find a clue that will help you to solve one of the mysteries revealed in the final chapter of the book.

"If you can't do great things, do small things in a great way."

—Napoleon Hill

A LETTER TO MY CHILDREN

Before I met your mother, life was all about me. The world revolved around me until God sent me the two of you. Only then did I finally understand how parenthood changes a person. Suddenly, the greatest joy in my life became seeing joy in your eyes. I made a silent vow to always protect you against the evils in this world. I am so blessed to be your father and thank God for you, the most amazing gift that I have ever been given. I can only hope that I will have as much impact on your life as you have already had on mine. Watching you learn and grow has easily been the greatest experience of my life. My darling children, I hope that by my example I have taught you to celebrate the beauty in diversity. Men and women from all backgrounds and ethnicities are created equal. Respect and appreciate the differences in others that give passion, creativity and variety to the world. I want you to have love, joy, peace, patience, kindness, goodness, faithfulness, gentleness, forgiveness, and self-control in your heart. Martin Luther King, Jr. said, "Whatever affects one directly, affects all indirectly. I can never be what I ought to be until you are what you ought to be, and you can never be what you ought to be until I am what I ought to be... This is the inter-related structure of reality". I'm not sure parenting ever gets easier, but I'm sure it will always be rewarding. No matter how difficult or unpredictable life is, you always put a smile on my face. You are the reason I persevere to get through the tough times. You are my motivation for everything. I'm grateful every day of my life for you. I hope you follow your heart and always do what you believe is right. Never falter to the pressures of others' beliefs. You are loved. Every single day, you're loved. Have dreams for yourself, your family and your country. Pursue those dreams and work hard to realize them. If hard work is not enough, then fight. William Bennett said, "Real fatherhood means love, commitment, sacrifice, a willingness to share responsibility and not walking away from one's children." My biggest wish in this life is that you are truly happy and comfortable with the choices you've made in your life. Enrich your life with happiness by helping the less fortunate. I wish for you a vocation that you love and that is fulfilling. Never forget that a lot of people are not as lucky as you and be as generous and as charitable as you can. I wish you all the love in the world. And just as it is my duty to encourage you to work hard and always give the best of yourself, it is also my job to tell you to enjoy the pleasures and learn from the mistakes you will make. One day, when you're very old, I want you to look back and say, "Lord, what a beautiful life I have lived."

With love,

Dad

P.S. Always remember December 6, 1865.

CONTENTS

IN THE BEGINNING, The man and his wife hear the sound of the Lord God as he was walking in the garden in the cool of the day, and they hid from the trees of the garden. But the Lord called to the man.

"Where are you?"

"I heard you in the garden, and I was afraid because I was naked, So I hid." Adam replies

The Lord God asks him "Who told you that you were naked? Have you eaten from the tree that I commanded you not to eat from?"

"The woman you put here with me, She gave me some fruit from the tree, and I ate it" Adam replies.

The Lord God said to the woman "What is this you have done?"

"The serpent deceived me, and I ate." Eve replies.

The Lord God said to the woman " I will make your pains in childbearing very severe, with painful labor you will give birth to children. Your desire will be for your husband and he will rule over you."

The Lord God said to the man "Because you listened to your wife and ate fruit from the tree about which I commanded you not to eat. Cursed is the ground because of you. Through painful toil you will eat food from it all the days of your life. It will produce Thorns and thistles for you, and you will eat the plants of the field by the sweat of your brow you will eat your food until you return to the ground, since from it you were taken from dust and to dust you will return."

PRESENT DAY, Tom Wilson, a 56-year-old news anchor, reports live from his network's studio in Washington, D.C. Behind him, a large screen displays a room inside the U.S. Capital building.

"The room is empty now, but in a few hours history will be made here," Tom begins as he addresses millions of viewers worldwide. "Congress will cast a vote to oust the President of the United States. Immediately afterwards, at nine p.m. Eastern time, the Chief Justice will likely swear in the Speaker of the House as our new leader and Commander in Chief. Just two days ago in a closed-door hearing President Fitzgerald testified in front of nine members of a congressional committee. We don't know exactly what was said, but we do know that most members of Congress, including members from his own party, wish to remove him from power. They believe that Fitzgerald is so unstable that he will drive our country into a third World War.

A few supporters, mostly evangelicals, think Fitzgerald will be able to retain his position. The presidential election is just three days away. According to the most recent polls, the president is losing by twenty five to thirty points. By all accounts the speaker will become president-elect in a few days time. Congress is speeding up the process because of what's been happening in that Kentucky Courthouse. Let's go live outside the courthouse. Our correspondent Sean Davis is there. Sean, can you hear me?"

The reporter, Sean Davis responds, "Loud and clear, Tom. There must be over ten thousand people here, but it's surreal. It feels like a ghost town. There's a group of people singing a hymn. You can see the worry on people's faces. Some are reading from Bibles under umbrellas, others are praying. They are praying, they say, to ask God for forgiveness. Some are fasting and haven't eaten in days.

It's almost noon on this rainy Friday and it's the last weekend before Tuesday's presidential election. Any minute now we should know the verdict. A few days ago the governor deployed National Guard troops to prevent others from joining this crowd. Today, even those who live in the city won't be likely to get back to their homes if they're away. Tom, it's amazing, there hasn't been one arrest. The people here, and around the world, are hoping to see the miracle that professor Samuel Doe foretold when he was on the witness stand; the miracle he claims will happen after the verdict is read.

Decades ago, we called the O.J. Simpson trial "the trial of the century," but according to professor Doe, this trial is a Biblical one in which the verdict is already written in the book of life."

Tom let's Sean finish, then offers,

"We think that most people expect a guilty verdict. But I want to go outside the box and ask you, Sean. What about you? Do you think Jason White will be found guilty of murder?

Sean, looking thoughtful responds, "First, I want to remind everyone that the judge presiding acted very intelligently. He realized the magnitude of this trial and ordered the jury to be sequestered. Just two weeks ago only people from this small town knew professor Doe. But now presidents as well as millions of people around the world would like to shake his hand and to talk with him because they so believe in him. They believe what he said on the stand- that he is the messenger of Jesus Christ. Today, after the verdict, they believe we will see the miracle that was foretold almost two hundred years ago. According to Doe, we will realize the greatness of Jesus Christ, know that he is the Son of God, and learn that one cannot go to the Father but through Him. Professor Doe read a letter on the stand; a letter he says was written by one of his ancestors. He stated, under oath, that the miracle about to happen would show the people of this world and the children of Abraham that Jesus is what He said He is. Doe recalls the promise God made to Abraham and therefore, his children need to begin giving glory to the Messiah. The jury isn't even aware of all the people anxiously awaiting the outcome of this decision. The answer to your question, Tom is "No". I believe the jury will find Jason White 'not guilty'.

Tom responds quickly,

"Sean, I'm surprised to hear that but I have to switch to the White House now as we have breaking news.

Folks, we just heard the President was just seen running from the White House. He boarded Marine One apparently on route to catch a flight on Air Force One, to an unknown destination. We have the video for you now. Here is the President running out– almost like he's trying to escape.

This just in– the stock market has taken an incredible plunge and the government has ordered the market to close. It's losing too much money, and they're trying to avoid a recession.

So many things are happening right now, we can barely keep up. Next up is a live feed from North Korea. War is starting again between North Korea and South Korea. In China the premier told his people that he doesn't know what kind of game the United States is playing, but if they invade Chinese airspace, it will be war and everything will be on the table, including nuclear warfare. Let's go to Pyongyang, the North Korean Capitol."

A North Korea spokesperson begins,

"Our leader will meet with the Chinese premier within hours at an undisclosed location. He sends this message to the world, "Years ago, the agreement that was made with the Trump administration is no longer valid. The way we saw this current American President run out like a coward, and we realize there is no turning back. War is inevitable. Our military planes are already in the sky. We are resuming the fight for our birth right until both Koreas are united under my supreme leadership."

Back at the courthouse in D.C., Judge Hamilton addresses the foreman of the jury, "Have you reached a verdict?"

The jury foreman replies,

"Yes, your honor."

Judge Hamilton casts his gaze up the defendant and instructs,

"Jason White, Please stand. Jury foreman please read the verdict."

The jury foreman stands and addresses the court,

"We, the jury, find the defendant, Jason White…"

Meanwhile at the exact time the verdict is being read, a massive explosions rock a high-rise building near the center of downtown Seoul, South Korea. Inside, hundreds of people are working, and living. Miles away the multiple explosions can be heard as the building collapses after a missile strike.

ONE-YEAR PRIOR, A football game is in progress between the Monroe Lions and a competing high school. The Lions are facing a higher-ranked team, the Eagles. Professor Samuel Doe, his wife Paula, and their daughter Chelsea sit in the bleachers watching Daniel Doe, quarterback; play his last high school game. Chelsea's ex-boyfriend, Mike, struts a few steps below, holding his new girlfriend's hand and kissing her. He steals glances at Chelsea, hoping to make her jealous.

Chelsea leans toward her mother, "Mom, he is so pathetic, parading that girl around in front of me. It was his womanizing that made me dump him."

A Reporter for the ESPN sports network is in attendance, covering the story of Daniel Doe, as many of the nation's top colleges have been trying to recruit Daniel. Daniel has turned them all down, including West Point.

Daniel throws a long pass to his team's fullback. An opposing player tries to intercept, but fails. The fullback catches the pass. Another opponent takes Daniel down, but the team gains twenty yards. The crowd cheers and Daniel's family applauds.

The center hikes the ball to Daniel, who hands it off to a halfback who passes it back to Daniel, Daniel dodges around an opposing tackle and another opposing player. Daniel takes off down field. Eagles players try for a tackle but Daniel weaves around and through them to run in a touchdown!

Daniel's family leaps from their seats and the fans cheer wildly.

Those nearest him can hear the reporter exclaim, "An amazing run! We see shades of the famous runner Barry Sanders in this young player. The fans are chanting Daniel's name. We can only hope that once his military obligation is over, he will sign with a professional team. This amazing athlete scored over fifty points in a basketball game in his freshman year. Such talent comes once in a lifetime."

The scoreboard shows two and a half minutes remaining on the clock. The score is forty-eight to forty seven in favor of the Lions.

The Eagles are in possession of the ball. Their quarterback, nearly tackled twice, unloads a pass to his wide receiver for a first down. On their next play they score a touchdown to regain the lead, but the kicker misses the extra points. Now the scoreboard shows the Eagles leading by five points with only thirty seconds left on the clock. The Eagles players and their fans cheer wildly, celebrating their probable victory. Some of the Lions fans even leave their seats.

Daniel reassures his teammates, "We've got time for another play."

The Lions take the offensive. Five players race down the field, flooding one area in the end zone and wait.

Daniel takes the snap and moves backward. An Eagles lineman chases Daniel out of pocket. Daniel throws the ball from his own thirty-five yard line.

The ball sails through the afternoon sky. As it begins to descend over the players' heads, they leap, but the ball sails right between their arms, just past the tips of their fingernails and falls behind them, right into the arms of a wide receiver.

The referee raises his arms in the air to indicate a touchdown. No one can believe it. The Lions players race off their sideline onto the field, towards the end zone. They lift Daniel to their shoulders and carry him in front of the home team's bleachers.

Again, the reporter can be heard, "Can you believe what we've just witnessed?"

Three

THE LOCAL PIZZERIA is hosting the Lions' victory celebration. Raucous cries are heard throughout the small establishment.

Professor Samuel Doe drives his family into the busy parking lot. He pulls into a spot near the front entrance very recently marked 'Reserved for Daniel'.

Dozens of screaming fans sing the school's fight song. Others yell praise for Daniel. As Daniel climbs out of the car, people ask him for his autograph.

Daniel enters the pizzeria, followed by his family. A big poster of Beyonce lemonade on the wall in the front entrance. The music stops. People scream. The crowd chants a request for Daniel to speak. The Lions' coach steps up onto a chair and shouts, "Mayors, governors and presidents will come and go, but Daniel's name will always be in our hearts and in the hearts of our children. What happened on that football field today will always be remembered as long as our city stands. Now let's hear from the man of the century."

The coach gets down from the chair. Daniel takes his place. The fans are screaming his name "Daniel, Daniel, Daniel…"

The quarterback looks a little emotional and says, "Tonight God was on our side. We could have beaten any team in the world. I don't like to brag, but how could I be bragging when I am speaking the truth?" He raises his arms and continues, "Let's all say, 'God is with us. Therefore we are the best!'"

The crowd repeats, "God is with us. Therefore we are the best!"

Daniel shouts "Again!" and the crowd obliges. "Again!" And the crowd is all too happy to repeat the chant. Daniel, smiling and looking pleased says, "Now let's eat!"

People eat pizza, drink sodas and talk among themselves. Becky, the beautiful head cheerleader, approaches Daniel's table and addresses him,

"Danny, this is ridiculous, I've been waiting for you for way too long. I heard you're leaving soon. Don't you want a girl like me to be here waiting for you? Chelsea's mom, Paula, whispers to her "Who is that?"

Chelsea replies, "That's Becky, the girl with the good hair."

"What?" asks Paula, looking puzzled.

Chelsea stands, excuses herself and heads toward the bathroom.

Daniel answers Becky, "Becky, I never asked you to wait for me. I've told you before, my heart belongs to someone else. Even though she's not here tonight, I know I'll be with her soon."

"You're the big football hero tonight", Becky counters, "How could you be so stupid? Don't answer that. Just watch me walk away from you. Daniel doesn't look her way. Instead, he looks towards the other side of the room and spots Chelsea's ex-boyfriend, seemingly harassing her. He jumps up from the table and approaches his sister and Mike.

"Is there a problem?" he asks pointedly.

"It's okay, Danny", Chelsea responds, "There is a pig in front of me trying to talk to me. But believe me, big brother, it's not a pit bull. A pig I can handle."

Daniel smiles and heads back to his table. Daniel reassures his parents,

"Everything is okay. Chelsea's not a little girl. She can take care of herself." Chelsea confronts Mike. "What do you mean, give you another chance? It's not something that happened once. You've been lying to me and to yourself for months. That's why I will never forgive you. I hope tonight is the last time you and I will ever speak to each other."

Mike pleads with Chelsea, "The other girls don't mean anything to me. You are and will always be the one for me! I was just trying to make you jealous." I didn't know what else to do." He steps closer to her.

"Maybe I need my brother's help after all, because you are a heavy pig."

She stalks away and returns to her family's table.

CHAPTER Four

PRESIDENT FITZGERALD, IN the Oval Office sits at his desk, and addresses his campaign staff, "You are all doing a great job with my reelection campaign. Keep up the good work!"

Linda, his secretary, opens the door and announces, "Your wife and daughter have arrived home, sir." and closes the door.

"My two favorite people are finally home." states the president. "Hopefully the American people will see how much happier I am now. That should count for a few more points in our favor." Everyone in the room chuckles at this notion.

Linda returns, "Pastor Raphael is waiting."

"I asked you not to make the Pastor wait. Everybody out and get back to work. Remember, the American people chose me once, and they are going to choose me again, not the Speaker of the House."

The staff exits the room as Linda ushers in Pastor Raphael. The president greets him with a big smile, "Pastor Raphael."

"Mr. President, always an honor and a pleasure to see you." replies the pastor.

"Don't flatter me, Pastor. You know how much I need your advice and your wisdom these days. I had that dream again last night. It didn't feel like a dream. It felt just like I am talking to you right now."

The Pastor replies "Was it the same one or…"

"Here I am, the President of the United States, sitting in the big chair in the Oval Office, confiding in you about my dreams. If the people learn about this, they will send me straight from the White House and into the nut house!"

The President gestures for the Pastor to sit down and continues,

"You've never doubted me, I can see in your face that you believe what I've told you. For that, I'm very grateful. My family should be here any minute, before I talk to my wife, please pray with me, Pastor." They rise from their chairs, kneel on the floor, and fold their hands in prayer.

The pastor starts, "Dear Lord, please guide President Fitzgerald in his hour of need. Help him to understand Your will and to follow it faithfully. Amen."

The men rise. The President looks the pastor in the eyes.

"Amen. Thank you very much for coming, Pastor."

As the president opens the door for the pastor, the First Lady, Rita and their seven-year-old daughter, Sophie rush into the room. Sophie runs into her father's waiting arms.

"Dad, guess what I missed most, besides you."

"Your friends?" he guesses.

"School! It just so happens that my friends are there too."

They both laugh and Fitzgerald says "I have a surprise for you. I'll see you in a little while, upstairs."

As Sophie exits the room, Rita hugs and kisses her husband.

"Rita, my love. How are you?" he asks as he leads her to the sofa.

"Babe, what I am about to tell you might make you think I'm crazy."

"You're scaring me, George. But I would never think you're..."

"Since you left I've been having the same dream over and over. The one last night was so real, I thought I was really awake, talking to an angel of God."

"What was his message?" she asks. What does God want us to do?"

"He said I've been chosen to lead this country through what will soon happen. He also blessed our family. He told me I will win the election and that the margin of victory will be the biggest in history. He also said that the bed I am sleeping in will not only be my bed for the next five years, but for the next thirteen years. Because I will still be living in the White House."

The first lady hugs him.

"How is that possible?" She asks.

"After the first dream I called Pastor Raphael. He made me realize that God has chosen me and that he has chosen you to succeed me."

"Me? President? I'm not a politician. Still, if God has chosen me, then I will answer his call. We need to let the American people know that we have God on our side."

He hugs her. She embraces him back, and then pulls away.

"The critics will call you unstable, crazy," she says "but let them use everything in their arsenal because we know who's in our corner."

President Fitzgerald stands up, pushes a button on the intercom and speaks,

"Linda, I have an announcement about my campaign. Call Wolf at CNN."

Professor Doe and his wife and daughter are driving Daniel to the bus station. Daniel has his backpack on the seat beside him. His mother turns to him and speaks,

"Daniel, you're not eighteen yet. You can change your mind right now and go to West Point instead."

Daniel shakes his head.

"No matter how many times you tell me that you want to start from the bottom, there is absolutely nothing wrong if someone puts you in the middle of the ladder and you climb up from there," she continues.

"Mom, I've made a commitment. Since I was little, I always said that after high school, this is what I wanted to do, not go to West Point or any other school." Paula turns around in her seat and continues,

"You need to earn a college degree!"

"I will finish my education." Daniel counters. "I really don't see myself doing anything else right now. This is my calling! We're at war with the terrorists. I may be in harm's way, but this is my life."

The car pulls into the bus station. Daniel hugs his mother and father. His sister presents him with a bracelet and quietly speaks. "I want this back, bro, when you come back home. Just hold onto it for me because it's my favorite piece of jewelry. You gave yours away to that girl you think is the love of your life and you don't even know where she is anymore."

Daniel embraces her then moves toward the bus. He blows kisses to his family and shouts, "Best family ever! Love you guys!"

A CNN CAMERA crew fills the Blue Room on the first floor of the White House. Wolf Levine, a CNN broadcast journalist, addresses the President, "Mr. President. This is really unexpected. Your people called us regarding an announcement you'd like to make about your reelection."

Wolf turns to the First Lady and continues, "First of all, we at CNN would like to welcome you back home, Mrs. Fitzgerald, from the successful humanitarian trip you and your daughter made to Africa."

Rita smiles and nods to Wolf. "Thank you, Wolf."

Wolf turns back to the President. "I am going to acknowledge the elephant in the room, Sir. Rumor has it that you are going to withdraw your nomination for reelection because you're so far behind in the polls. You do realize there is no way you can win?"

"Let me stop you right there, Wolf." interjects Fitzgerald, "The only reason that I'm here is to tell the American people that not only will I win reelection, but I will win every state in our great nation."

Wolf, astonished, responds, "Mr. President, how can you say that to the American people? Do you really believe what you're saying? People will suggest that you're unstable, and not fit to be Commander in Chief."

Fitzgerald responds, "Wolf, do you believe in our savior, Jesus Christ?"

"No, sir, I'm Jewish." Wolf replies.

Fitzgerald asks, "Do you believe in God?"

"Of course I do" Wolf tells him. "What are you saying, Mr. President? Are you telling the American people that God has informed you that you will take all fifty states?"

The President pauses and reaches for his wife's hand and responds, "Yes, he did. He also said the time is coming when He will need me to lead the American People."

The president and his wife exchange supportive looks. He continues, "Millions of people pray, and go to church, and they see miracles every day. If we simply look at ourselves in the mirror, or witness all of His wonders by stepping outside and looking to nature…" He points out the window at the stately trees and continues,

"But when I repeat what he told me, most people will doubt it. I am not unstable. If you doubt what I am saying right now, you are also doubting Him."

"Are you talking about God or Jesus Christ?" asks Wolf.

"I believe Jesus is the Son of God. The Son is in the Father, and the Father is in the son."

"We'll leave it to the American people to decide your fate." finishes Wolf.

The White House Chief of Staff is working damage control. The Press Secretary steps to the podium and speaks into the microphone answering the questions that at hurling at him, "No, no. The president didn't have a conversation with God. He meant God and his son inspire him."

The president strides into the room, takes over the podium, and addresses the reporters that are gathered.

"I meant every word I said in that interview tonight. There won't be anything else to add right now."

Most of the journalist ignore him and whisper to each other. They are looking on their tablets, watching Glen Washington, the Speaker of the House. Annoyed, the president leaves the room.

Speaker Washington addresses them, "What we've just witnessed in that interview is evidence that the President of the United States is an unstable leader. For the good of the country I hope he will resign and let Vice President Webster take over the office and also replace him on the ticket as his party's candidate."

All of the reporters are now staring at their tablets.

"There is no way I can lose to that guy– is there?" Washington continues. "I will answer my own question. Heck, no!"

The Journalists look at each other and nod in agreement with the Speaker.

"Before that interview I was already more than twenty points ahead. Now, I am sure Americans cannot wait to kick him out of office. We now know just how unstable he is. That makes him the most dangerous man alive. Tomorrow morning, after I speak with my colleagues, we will begin impeachment proceedings."

Six

A BLACK SEDAN approaches the Doe family home and pulls up curbside. Two uniformed servicemen exit the car and walk towards the front door. In the living room, Professor Doe and his daughter dance to the Luther Vandross song, "Dance with My Father". The Professor's wife is carrying in a pitcher of lemonade that she's just made as the doorbell rings. Professor Doe, laughing, turns off the music and opens the door. The two military men stand in front of him holding Chelsea's bracelet. Paula drops the pitcher and falls to the floor. Chelsea runs into her father's arms.

"The United States Army and our entire country are very sorry about your son, your brother, and also our brother," the first serviceman states.

"He died saving another soldier." The second man continues, "He pushed him out of the way and was hit instead. A true American hero."

"A note in his pocket said... In case something happens to me, make sure my sister gets this bracelet back." the first man offers.

"When will my son's body come home?" Professor Doe asks somberly.

"Tomorrow evening, sir," one of the servicemen states.

"Thank you." the professor says. He closes the door after the men depart and returns to the living room, drops to the floor beside his wife and takes her in his arms. Together, with Chelsea, they sob all night long.

CHAPTER

Seven

PRESIDENT FITZGERALD'S CHIEF of Staff runs into the Oval Office. A meeting is in session.

"Mr. President, Mr. President. Your daughter…" begins the Chief of Staff.

The president rises to his feet at once. "What about my daughter?" he demands.

"She's very sick. The First Lady is with her now."

"What the heck are you talking about? Fitzgerald demands. "Where is she? She was perfectly fine this morning."

The President follows his Chief of Staff outside and they climb into the President's waiting automobile.

The Chief of Staff continues, "She's at Bethesda Hospital sir. We received a call from the Nigerian Embassy. One of the little girls your daughter played with in Africa died from an Ebola-like disease. We called her school to check on Sophie. The nurse told us she was exhibiting symptoms similar to what we heard the Nigerian girl experienced. Mr. President, I'm afraid the news is much worse."

"What could be worse? What aren't you telling Me. Tell me everything you know." demanded Fitzgerald.

"She might be contagious, sir. Not only that, but if she's positive, this disease could kill her within days" the Chief of Staff explained.'

The President doesn't say another word until they arrive to the Hospital. They run inside trailed by an army of Secret Service agents. Inside a glass isolation room, the First Lady, wearing a HAZMAT suit, cradles her daughter.

Also tending to the patient are nurses and doctors, all wearing protective gear. The president tries to enter but is stopped by Secret Service Agents. One of them points to a sign on the door that reads, 'WARNING: UNIDENTIFIED DISEASE'.

"Get out of my way! My daughter needs me." Shouts President Fitzgerald.

The Agents move out of his way except one who declares, "Sir, it's for your own protection. I can't let you expose yourself, you must wear a suit."

"I gave you a direct order! You're fired!" shouts Fitzgerald.

"With all respect, it doesn't work that way, sir."

The two men struggle. The agent pushes the President up against the wall. He takes two steps back, pulls out his gun, and holds it to his own head. "Sir, I swore to protect you with my life, so if you go in there without protection, I will pull this trigger."

The phone at the nurse's station rings and is answered by the receptionist.

"Hello. Yes, I'll tell them right away."

She heads for the glass room, and speaks into the intercom. "It's chickenpox." Everyone breathes an exasperated sigh of relief.

The President addresses the Secret Service Agent. "I understand that you were just doing your job. Thank you. I always want you by my side."

"I appreciate that, sir," responds the agent.

He opens the door to the isolation room, and the President rushes inside and hugs his daughter and his wife.

CHAPTER

Eight

THE DOORBELL RINGS. The Does family and friends are inside getting ready to go to Daniel's funeral. Chelsea opens the door the postman gives her a letter from Daniel. She runs inside her bedroom to read it. Her mother can hear her crying and laughing.

"Are you okay honey?" Paula asks

Chelsea opens her door and embraces her mom.

"Mom, on this sorrow day, I received a letter from Danny. A beautiful letter that I will tell you about it's content later." Replies Chelsea.

Rita walks inside the presidential study room. President George Fitzgerald is on his knees with his eyes closed and an open arms.

"The Lord showed me what will soon happen. How marvelous! How divine! He is the truth! From dust God created us in his own image. There is a family that is going through so much pain right now and it's going to get so much worse for them much worse. Yet that family is so blessed much more than our family. That is how great our Lord is. I will not eat, drink or do anything else today. I will stay here and my mouth will only give glory to the almighty God." President Fitzgerald Says

At Daniel's funeral, many supportive neighbors and townspeople crowd outside the funeral home. Nearby protestors scream slogans against the government's policy to fight on foreign soil. A sign is seen that reads: "SCREW the army and its fake Sympathy". Several police officers are on the scene attempting to maintain order. The Doe family arrives with a military escort.

Professor Doe, his wife, and daughter enter the church. The family and their entourage take seats in the front row.

Chelsea sobs, "I'm too emotional. I don't think that I can do it."

"Just think of your brother, honey. You'll be fine," her mother advises.

Chelsea approaches the piano and seats in front of it. She stares at the keys for a moment that feels like an eternity. Finally, she begins to play Elton John's "Daniel". Most in attendance don't even know that Chelsea sings and plays and are astonished at her talent. She delivers an incredible and very moving rendition of the songs and once finished, she moves to the podium and speaks.

"The story of Adam and Eve's first children, Cain and Abel."

She looks over the congregation, still settling in their seats.

"Abel was a Shepherd and Cain, a farmer. At harvest time, Cain brought a gift to the Lord– food that he'd grown in the ground. But Abel brought sheep from his flock. The Lord accepted Abel's offering, but not Cain's. Cain grew angry. The Lord asked him, "Why are you angry? You know if you do what is right, I will accept you. But if you don't, sin is ready to claim you." Later, Cain took Abel to a field, where he attacked his brother and killed him. God loved Abel. God blessed Abel. And yet he let Cain kill him."

Mr. and Mrs. Doe are overcome with sobbing.

So whenever I dare to ask God, Chelsea continued, "Why did you let my brother die so young? I am reminded of the story of Cain and Abel. And I thank the almighty God because I know and my family knows that Daniel is in a better place. He is with God."

Professor Doe looks at his daughter with pride.

Later, at the cemetery, Daniel's coffin is centered over the gravesite. His family, friends and the military escort are gathered around. In the distance behind, a fence, the protesters continue to spew their hateful venom. Their leader is Howard White, a pastor known for his hate speech, especially against Blacks, Jews, the LGBT community, as well as politicians and the military. They hurl racial, religious and gender-biased slurs. Howard's son, Jason, climbs over the fence and sprints toward Daniel's casket. A policeman tries to intercept him, but Jason eludes his grasp and rushes the family.

Chelsea pulls out a pocketknife and attempts to stop him. Jason is too big for her. He overpowers her, grabs the knife, and stabs her in the neck. Professor Doe catches his daughter before she hits the ground. She manages a smile at her parents and says, "I don't feel anything, but I know that I'm dying. Don't worry. I'm on my way to be with Daniel in God's kingdom.

CHAPTER
Nine

LINDA CALLS PRESIDENT Fitzgerald on the intercom.

"Sir, the Vice President is here," she informs him.

A moment later Vice President Webster enters Fitzgerald's office.

The President doesn't even look up at Webster. He says only, "Sit down."

"I'd rather stand", replies Webster.

The President glares at him. "I know you've been running behind my back, trying to get enough votes to impeach me. I'm sure by now you realize that you don't have the votes."

Webster looks incredulous as the President continues.

"Why sneak around? You should have been a man and come to me. I no longer trust you and cannot abide you as a running mate in re-election campaign."

Webster laughs. "What re-election? Are you kidding me? You're the captain of the Titanic. Everyone knows what's going to happen. We hit an iceberg."

President Fitzgerald jumps to his feet while Webster continues,

"Don't worry, Mr. President, I'm getting off your ship right now. As of today, I am announcing my resignation and changing my party to independent. I talked to the Speaker, who assures me I will have a place in his cabinet."

"You fool", retorts Fitzgerald. "Don't you think he needs to win the job first before he can select Members of a fictitious Cabinet?"

"Perhaps you should follow my lead and resign yourself. But you are too stubborn to do that. Do you really think that you can win re-election, when you probably won't even last to the end of your first term?" barks Webster.

"You will be sorry, for what you are about to do, that much I can guarantee you!" asserts the President.

Webster shouts his response, "Everyone knows you're going to do something incredibly stupid before your terms ends. Whomever you pick as my replacement will be kicked out as well. The Speaker will become President even before the election. You're done George!"

"Get out!" shouts the President.

As Vice President Webster heads for the door he says "One last chance. I'm giving you a way out. Resign now. Lead the people that want to follow you by doing something as a private citizen. Moses wasn't a king, but he did lead his people to the Promised Land."

As Webster exits the room, the President shouts after him, "I accept your resignation. Good day, sir!"

Ten

SPEAKER WASHINGTON AND his Chief of Staff, Marvin Mason, are watching the news on a television screen. The newscaster states, "We have just learned that the Vice President is resigning his office. Additionally, he will switch his party affiliation to Independent and join Speaker Washington's campaign for President" Washington addresses Mason. "Great job, Marvin. Fitzgerald's position is looking less and less tenable every day. Anyone who wants a future in politics won't run on his ticket."

Marvin nods in agreement while the Speaker continues.

"The obvious move for him will be to have his wife as the new vice president. But when he's impeached, she'll go down with him. So it looks like I'll be President sooner rather than later."

Moving to a side table with liquor bottles and glassware, Washington unscrews the cap from a bottle of whiskey and continues, "We have the majority in Congress, and so we will not approve anyone but his wife to replace the fool Webster as VP. Let us drink, my friend."

Mason replies, "Let us drink in your honor, Mr. President. The press is already calling you the soon–to–be president-elect but sir, you and I know you will be president even before the election. Therefore I want to be the first one to call you Mr. President."

"I like the sound of that!" beams Washington.

"So this drink is for you, sir.", says Marvin as he raises his drink. Both men laugh and take swallows of their drinks.

The Press Secretary stands on the podium in the pressroom. Marvin Mason turns up the volume on the television. The Press Secretary begins, "The President of the United States doesn't want anyone other than his wife, Rita, to be his Vice President, so he will nominate her to be his running mate."

Washington and Marvin nod to each other.

CHAPTER

MIKE AND HIS girlfriend, Valeska are in a cab caught in a traffic jam. Mike is speaking on the phone with his brother, Ethan.

"Hey bro. The traffic sucks, but we'll be there soon."

"What do you mean we?" Ethan replies. The phone has gone dead.

"Mike, are you still there?"

Annoyed, he clicks off the phone and tosses it on the coffee table. He moves to a plate glass window and stares out. He then switches on the television and turns to a news channel. Ethan Black is a successful attorney in New York City.

There is a knock on the door. Ethan lowers the sound of the television and opens the door to his brother Mike and Mike's girlfriend.

"Hey, bro. Hi, Valeska. Come on in."

Mike, admiring the place, exclaims, "Park Avenue, black leather sofas, and a lavish living room. Looks like you're pretty successful, bro. Awesome!"

Mike plops down on the leather sofa. Valeska wanders over to a sideboard, where she toys with appetizer. Ethan pointedly ignores her and speaks to his brother.

"It's been almost a year since you graduated from High School. Dad asked me to talk to you regarding your future because it seems like all you are doing amounts to a big nothing."

Valeska sighs as Mike begin his defense.

"Bro, not everybody needs to be like you. I'm trying to find myself. Life is short and I want to travel Europe with Valeska."

Valeska strolls over and sits down next to Mike. He pats her leg and continues, "The food smells great. Is it almost ready?"

Noelle, Ethan's girlfriend, enters from the kitchen and approaches the guests. Smiling, she says, "Nice to finally meet you, Mike. And, yes, the food is ready."

The television is on and a newscaster is heard announcing, "Here is the latest on the prosecution versus Jason White. Next Monday he will take a plea bargain, so there won't be a trial."

Ethan silences the TV. They all move into the dining room and take places around the table. Noelle brings out several dishes.

Ethan breaks the silence. "I'm so sorry, bro. I know you were friends with Chelsea. I do feel for that family because they've lost both of their children. Dad told me about it."

Mike responds, "She was wrong about her brother"

"What do you mean?" asks Ethan.

"She once told me she saw her father give her brother a letter, telling him it's for his eyes only. It has been passed down from generation to generation, only to the first born." Mike explains.

Ethan stands up, furious with his brother and shouts, "What are you telling me? dad and I told you that if you ever saw or heard anything regarding that family while you and Chelsea were dating, to let us know. Didn't you think that was important to tell us? What else did she say?"

Mike, sheepish, responds, "She didn't know what was in the letter because her brother lied when she asked him about it the next day.

As the carrier of that letter, He will need to give it to his firstborn. Apparently, God's justice comes before family."

Ethan excuses himself and leaves the dining room. He picks up his cell phone to call his father.

"Dad, it's a letter the Doe family has been passing around for generations. We need to find out what's in it. I'm coming home right now before it's too late to be Jason White's defense attorney."

Ethan hangs up and returns to the dining room where he again, addresses his brother. "For years now, I have envied you, little brother because you don't have a care in the world."

Mike looks surprised as Ethan continues.

"Don't you ever ask yourself…? No, I don't imagine you do. Why, for generations, has someone in our family always been a lawyer or judge? I truly believe if I didn't become an attorney, dad would have killed me and made sure you'd become one."

Mike, Valeska and Noelle exchange looks as Ethan continues, "I'm not exaggerating." He begins circling the table as he speaks. "I was fifteen years old when dad showed me an old letter from our great, great grandfather. That thing must've been over two hundred years old. It's vague, but the message is clear."

He stops behind Noelle's chair as he announces, "The first born must be an attorney. He is a watchman until the day comes when he can expose the Doe family's secret to the world in a court of law."

Ethan fixes his eyes on Mike and implores, "Now you're telling me that family really does have a secret that they are even keeping from each other. To me, it's a legend, a fairy tale, but dad said he was feeling the same way I do now until, he had me, his first child. That letter also says failing to do what is written will result in a curse for that person and his children. The next sibling should be the watchman. I know what I must do now for the sake of my unborn children."

As he heads for the bedroom, he turns back, addresses the seated group, and says, "Mike and Valeska, you can stay as long as you want and enjoy Noelle's delicious food. She and I are going to dad's place right now. I don't fly, so we'll be driving. Hon, you're finally going to visit the place where I grew up."

"What do you mean?" Mike asks.

"Little bro, I cannot say too much right now but you will soon find out because I'm on my way to defend Jason White. There is one more thing I can tell you. That letter is real, and I intend to find out what's in it. Our family has been trying to find out what the Doe's have been hiding for generations."

On the TV the words "Breaking News' flash on and off the screen. Ethan turns up the sound. They all pay attention to the report.

The newscaster announces, "For the first time in our country's history, we have a President and Vice President who are husband and wife. Mrs. Fitzgerald has just been sworn in as our country's V.P. She faced no challenge on the Senate floor. They approved the president's nomination without debate."

CHAPTER

Twelve

ETHAN, NOELLE, AND Ethan's parents, Seth and Juliette Black are climbing into Ethan's Mercedes Benz. He turns the engine key on to start the car but it does not start.

"I really don't understand what's going on, this is a brand new car and it's full of gas."

A crow on top of the fence is staring at them. Mr. and Mrs. Black get out of the car so they can take their car instead but it won't start either.

Ethan's parents look on as Ethan checks under the hood of his car."

The elder Black's live in a big farmhouse and there is no help immediately at hand. Ethan is upset and slams the hood of the car. They all gaze toward the fences to see that crows that seem to be staring at them surround them.

Ethan pleads, "Guys, go inside. I'm going to make a run for it, that's the only chance that I have to make it on time before the court accepts Jason's guilty plea."

"Wait", cries Ethan's father. "You won't make it on time."

He runs inside the house while yelling, "I'll be back!"

The Crows look like they are about to launch at them when a big thunderclap sounds from the sky above. They all look up to the sky and look again toward the fences. The crows have scattered.

Seth rushes out of the house with a bicycle, shouting, "Ethan, use this."

Ethan walks back to his car and says calmly, "I have a feeling it's going to start now."

Ethan climbs inside the car and the engine starts without issue. The others look on in disbelief.

Thirteen

A CORRECTIONAL DEPARTMENT Van carrying Jason White is slowing down because a throng of people is in the street shouting and throwing eggs at the van. Cries of "Murderer", "Coward", and "You are going to hell!" can be heard.

The courthouse is full. Jason White and his lawyer sit to the left of the prosecutor, Donald Carson. Howard White and his wife sit in the row behind their son.

Judge Arnold Hamilton, an African American man, begins to proclaim Jason's indictment. "Jason White, you stand accused of murdering miss Chelsea Doe. Do you understand the charges?"

"Yes, your honor." Jason replies, calmly.

"It's my understanding you wish to accept the plea bargain offered by the state to serve ten years in prison. Do you accept this plea?" continues the judge.

"Yes, your honor." replies Jason again.

"Knowing that you will not be able to change your mind; do you still accept this plea?" asks the judge.

Before Jason can answer, Ethan Black strides confidently into the courtroom and calls out, "No, your honor, he does not."

There is a collective gasp from the families and spectators, who turn to stare at the newcomer. Ethan stops at the defense table.

"You are disrupting my courtroom. Who are you?" demands the judge.

"Your honor, I'm Jason's new attorney, Ethan Black." announces Ethan.

Ethan approaches Howard White, and whispers in his ear,

"I have ten thousand dollars in cash in this briefcase. It's yours if you go along with me. I also believe that I can get your son off with no jail time and my services are free."

Howard White stands and addresses the court, "Your honor, my son was seventeen years old when he was accused. He has the right to obtain the best possible attorney. This gentleman is his new lawyer."

"The court will reconvene tomorrow so it can accept Jason White's plea." The judge declares, conceding to this abrupt change of direction.

"Your honor, my client is pleading 'not guilty,'" offers Ethan.

"Is this what you want, Mr. White?" asks Judge Hamilton.

Jason looks to his father, who nods his head.

Jason replies, "Yes, your honor."

"So be it. The trial will commence in two weeks, if you need an extension; file with the clerk within five business days."

"Thank you, your honor." Ethan offers, relieved. "Two weeks is more than enough time. We will be ready."

The spectators seem stunned by this unexpected turn.

Professor Doe takes his wife's hand and stands. He glares at Ethan, who stares back.

Fourteen

JASON, HIS FATHER, and Ethan enter a nearby anteroom.

Jason grabs his father's arm and pleads, "Dad, what the hell is going on? Who is this guy? People in this town hate us. They'll find me guilty, and I will get 'life'!"

"Relax, kid, I'm going to get you off. You should thank me," says Ethan. "Well, maybe later." Ethan says, looking incredulous.

"He gave us ten thousand dollars. That's how strongly he believes he can get you off." Howard offers.

"What?" Jason exclaims.

"Forget about the money, it's a gift that I gave you. You're right. The people here hate you. However, you are not guilty because she attacked you with a knife. You were defending yourself. So sit back and let me keep you out of prison."

Ethan moves toward Jason and gives him a piercing stare and continues to speak. "Do you believe me when I say I can get you off?"

Jason nods his head. "Yes"

Ethan grins. "Now the fun begins. We have to rid the jury of negative emotions and stick to the facts."

Fifteen

COURT IS IN session for Jason White's trial. Judge Hamilton is perched above the court on his bench. Ethan sits with Jason at the defense table. District attorney Carson and his prosecution team are at the adjacent table. Professor Samuel Doe, his wife, various townspeople, and others watch the proceedings. Potential jurors sit in the jury box. Ethan questions each one in turn, "Are you an atheist, Ma'am?" "Sir, Are you an atheist?"

Ethan approves those that say they are atheist. If they say they are not, he dismisses them. Ethan settles on five self-proclaimed atheists for the Jury. Finally he makes his opening statement. "In this trial a young man's life is on the line. I understand a young woman's life was taken away too soon. However, I will now present the facts about what happened on that unfortunate day."

Professor Samuel Doe and his wife exchange sorrowful looks as Ethan continues "Once all emotions are set aside, you will understand that my client acted in self-defense. The witnesses I've promised the court are no longer needed. I only have one witness to call for Jason White's defense.

"Your honor, I object. We don't know anything about this new witness," demands prosecutor Carson.

"Stop, stop, stop. I really don't like where this is going," states the judge. "I need to straighten things out. We will reconvene tomorrow morning."

The Judge addresses the jury. "Ladies and gentlemen of the jury, thank you very much. Have a good evening and sleep well. We will have a long day tomorrow." Judge Hamilton gestures to both attorneys. "I want the attorneys in my chambers."

"Your honor, I request that the victim's parents and the accused's parents also be there."

"Mr. Carson, any objections?" asks judge Hamilton.

Prosecutor Carson shakes his head. "No, your honor."

The attorneys, Mr. and Mrs. Howard White, and Professor Doe and his wife, Paula, stand before the judge in his chambers.

"Mr. Black, this is not New York, and this is not the way we do things here. You're starting by hurting your client, not helping him."

Ethan begins to object, but the judge holds up his hand.

The judge continues "Why are you saying that you will not call the witnesses that you've already proposed to the court. And who is this new witness you are suggesting?"

"Your honor" Ethan answers, "I'm working nonstop for my client's best interest. In fact that's all I've been thinking about. I'm trying to figure out a way to give my client the best possible defense. That's why I wanted his parents here with us in this chamber right now."

Professor Doe and his wife Paula exchange concerned looks.

"I believe," continues Ethan, "the only way I can prove my client's innocence to the jury is by having the truth come from the victim's father's mouth."

Everyone looks incredulous.

"What?" exclaims the prosecutor.

Disturbed, Professor Doe shakes his head.

"Professor Doe, you are being subpoenaed right now to be the only witness for the defense at the trial of your daughter's alleged murder."

"Is this a joke?" demands judge Hamilton. "No one is laughing. What are you doing, Mr. Black? You cannot do this."

The Judge turns to Howard White. "Mr. White, you may wish to fire your attorney right now because if the jury finds your son guilty, you will not succeed with any appeal. You have a big decision to make."

"Your honor, I am not a comedian, and this not a joke. I want what's best for my client. I will call Professor Samuel Doe to the stand because he has in his possession a letter that was given to him by his father."

Professor Doe looks incredulous.

"With the contents of that letter, I will be able to prove to the jury that my client is innocent and that justice comes first," states Ethan.

Professor Doe remains silent, but tears stream down his face. His wife, Paula, grabs his hands.

"Sam, what is he talking about? What kind of letter is this? Is it the one that Chelsea received from Danny the day of his funeral? I could never find it!" pleads Mrs. Doe. "How do you know that the professor has such a letter? It doesn't matter anyway. I will not allow it." Demands the judge.

"Your honor, since he thinks the letter will help his client, I will read it for the jury. And so it begins, just like he said."

"Like who said, Sam?" pleads Mrs. Doe again.

Professor Doe faints and collapses on the floor. Paula Doe kneels beside her husband. Judge Hamilton calls for help over his intercom and approaches the fallen man urging, "Stand back, everyone, help is on the way."

Professor Doe opens his eyes and speaks. "I'm okay. I just want to go home." The Judge looks worried.

"Do we need to postpone the trial for a few days?" asks the judge.

Professor Doe locks eyes with Ethan and responds. "No, your honor, I will be ready tomorrow. We have been waiting for almost two centuries for this, so I will not delay it, not for one more day."

"Your honor, the jury might be influenced from the outside by what Professor Doe reads. I'm requesting that you to have them sequestered."

The Judge looks thoughtful.

"I am willing to pay for it, in the case that the city cannot afford it."

"Mr. Doe, I will see you on the stand tomorrow morning." exclaims the judge.

He then turns to Ethan. "As for you Mr. Black, I just moved to this city, but I've already done my research on you. From what I've heard, you were an arrogant little boy, and it seems like you haven't changed a bit. We can afford to pay for the jury to be sequestered. Now everyone get out!"

Sixteen

PROFESSOR SAMUEL DOE and his wife Paula are in bed sleeping. Mrs. Doe wakes up and turns on the light from her side of the bed. Realizing that her husband is sleeping, she gets up and walks inside her husband's study room. On top of his desk is the letter that professor Doe will read in court tomorrow.

Professor Samuel Doe wakes up with a screaming sound from his wife. He runs inside the study room and his wife is there screaming completely blind. Her eyes are red like fire. The Professor looks on his desk, realizes what just happened. He drops on his knees to pray.

"Lord of Abraham, David, John Doe and all the living. We are not perfect like you but you still love us and that's the reason that you sent your son to save us from sins. My Lord, I am your servant, I will always do what you ask of me. My wife has sin against you. Please God forgive her and by doing so you will take away some of that heavy load off my shoulder. We all have sinned and fall short of your glory" Professor prays

Professor Doe opens his eyes after praying these words and his wife has gotten her eyesight back.

They embrace and give thanks to the almighty God.

Prosecutor Carson is delivering his final statements. "You have heard the witnesses and received all of the relevant facts in this case.

We have shown that the defendant, Jason White, fatally stabbed Chelsea Doe. The prosecution rests its case."

"Mr. Black, you may call your witness for the defense." States Judge Hamilton.

"I call Professor Samuel Doe," replies Ethan.

Professor Samuel Doe rises from his seat and walks down the aisle holding a big folder to his chest. Everyone appears surprised and stares at him.

When he takes the witness stand, the officer of the court begins to swear Doe in by saying, "Please raise your right hand."

Professor Doe holds up his right hand but continues to clutch the folder.

"Do you solemnly swear to tell the truth, the whole truth and nothing but the truth, so help you God?" continues the officer.

"I do," states the professor as he lowers his hand.

Ethan steps up to question him, but then turns to face the jury and begins to explain the unusual circumstances. "Ladies and Gentlemen of the jury. You must be wondering why the victim's father is taking the stand for the defense. You will soon learn the reason and it is why Professor Doe's testimony is essential. Justice must prevail over emotions. My client simply reacted. He was defending himself, just like police officers and our military men and women do every single day."

Ethan then turns back to Professor Doe and begins his questioning. "Mr. Doe, you are a professor. You teach law at the university. Most people here in the community know you, admire you, and feel for your family. I am one of them, I might add. I should also mention that you were my favorite professor while I attended the university."

Professor Doe nods his head in acknowledgement.

"So before I ask your opinion..." Ethan continues.

"Objection, your honor." Interjects prosecutor Carson.

"Overruled. Please continue, Mr. Black," responds Judge Hamilton.

"Thank you, your honor," continues Ethan. "Professor Doe, you have in your possession a letter, I am very anxious to hear you read it for the jury. I don't know the contents, but I am sure that truth and justice will take precedence over emotions and family ties."

"Mr. Black, you were one of my brightest students, and I am not surprised that you are so successful. I applaud you in saying that truth and justice supersede emotions and family ties. Well said."

Ethan looks on smugly as professor Doe continues. "The letter that I will read for the jury is dated December 31, 1865. It's from my great grandfather, John. No one in my family knows about it, apart from my first-born, Daniel. The same honor that my grandmother gave to my father, and my father gave to me, I gave to my son on his sixteenth birthday.

There is no way that my son would have told anyone about it. I therefore assume that my daughter Chelsea must have mentioned it to your brother Mike, Mr. Black. She overheard the conversation between my son and I."

Ethan nods his head in affirmation.

"You see, ladies and gentlemen," continues the professor, "I couldn't know that the event foretold in the letter would happen in my lifetime, but God has a plan for us all."

Doe removes the letter from the folder he is clutching and begins to read from it. "My name is John, if you are reading this letter you must be my son or my grandchild. In any case you are my descendant. This letter is for your eyes only as Jesus Christ's Messenger until the time comes when the world will know of its existence."

He stops reading, takes a breath and looks out over the courtroom to his wife and its inhabitants, then continues, "People will learn about this letter and its contents during a court trial. After the verdict is read, the entire world will witness or hear tell of the miracle that Jesus Christ promised would occur."

Some jurors gasp, others shake their heads and Doe reads on, "I don't know what the miracle will be, but He said there will be birds in the sky dropping the glorious message to the Jewish people on the land that God gave them."

Several people smile, others frown as the professor reads, "This message will be delivered to other countries, including China and North Korea.

For being his Messenger, He promised that the children of the letter-bearer would witness His divine return to glory."

"Professor Doe," interjects Judge Hamilton, North Korea didn't become a country until 1945. You are telling us that this letter was written in 1865, eighty years prior."

"Judge Hamilton," asserts Doe, "I assure you, under oath, that my father had it in his possession years before North Korea became a country."

Those assembled in the courtroom cannot believe what they are hearing and begin whispering to each other, as do the jurors.

"Everyone, please quiet down," demands Judge Hamilton. "Members of the jury, kindly exit the courtroom."

The jurors file out. The Judge addresses Professor Doe, "Professor Doe, please explain this letter? Is this for real? Mr. Black, how do you know that the contents of this letter will help your client?"

"Your honor," responds Ethan, "It's true that I'm not aware of the exact contents of this letter, but I'm going with a gut feeling. I truly believe that whatever is in the letter will help me to prove that my client acted purely in self-defense."

Professor Doe responds, "Your honor, I assure you this letter is real. It's been with my family for almost two hundred years. My family is mourning, but the world should rejoice because soon we will all witness the glory of God."

"Please ask the Jury to return," the judge requests.

"I have a question for the witness, your honor," states prosecutor Carson.

The judge grants the request and Carson begins, "Professor Doe, you and your wife are advanced in age and both of your children are no longer with us. Why should we give any merit to this letter, when it says that your children will witness God's return to glory?"

"You're correct, regarding our age, especially mine, but I leave everything in Jesus' hands and soon you too will believe," asserts Doe.

The Jury members and spectators look bewildered and talk amongst themselves. The judge looks exasperated as he states, "All right, this court will recess until tomorrow when Professor Doe will resume reading the letter."

CHAPTER

Seventeen

TOM WILSON, NEWSCASTER, opens his broadcast as the words 'Breaking News' stream across his monitor. "All over the world people are talking about what's going on in the trial of Jason White. They all wonder what's in this mysterious letter, a letter that was written almost two hundred years ago.

In North Korea, the country's leader has said: If birds fly over their airspace to drop messages, they will kill and eat them. The Israeli Prime Minister has called on the Chinese Premier and asked him to issue a strong statement against the United States. According to most of these world leaders, President Fitzgerald seems to fear he will lose reelection. They believe Fitzgerald is desperate and looking for any means by which to resurrect his campaign."

A photo of the President appears behind Tom as he continues, "The Chinese have responded thus. If the President of the United States sends planes into Chinese airspace, it will be taken as an act of war. The Chinese leader has just released a statement confirming this."

Eighteen

PRESIDENT FITZGERALD STANDS with Anthony Delbois, the newly elected president of Haiti as photographers snap pictures. The press vies for the opportunity to ask questions.

"Haiti is our next door neighbor." President Fitzgerald begins, "From Florida we can reach that beautiful island within two hours. The world has been neglecting these people. As Americans we can do much more to help them. I have promised President Delbois that I will personally visit Haiti and bring a number of business executives with me. The goal is to help create an environment in which his people can live to their full potential."

"In order for that to happen, we need to see to it that the Haitian people have access to necessities. In short; adequate food, water, and shelter as well as healthcare and education."

Reporters shoot their hands into the air. The president ignores them as he continues; "We have also talked about the opportunity for them to compete economically with other Caribbean islands. They will need to build resorts and improve infrastructure. This will provide jobs for the Haitian People."

A Wall Street Journal reporter asks, "President Delbois, your people have heard this before. What do you believe is different about these new promises?"

"My country is at the bottom of the socioeconomic scale. We have been there for far too long. There is really no way to go but up. These are not the same old hollow promises because I can really see a bright future for my people."

A Washington Post reporter interjects; "The presidential election is just a few days away. Polls show that President Fitzgerald will not be reelected. Do you think he'll be able to keep his word if this comes to pass?"

"Your president assures me that I need not worry. He will not abandon our country, no matter what happens, and I truly believe him."

A New York Times reporter yells over the noise, "President Fitzgerald, we've just heard from the Associated Press regarding Jason's White's murder trial and the letter that everyone is talking about."

A CNN reporter interrupts, "China, North Korea, and Israel think that you're desperate to win reelection. So desperate you might send military planes to drop propaganda for political support. Those countries have released a joint statement saying that if you send planes into their airspace, it will be considered an act of war."

President Fitzgerald responds, "If God asked you to do something, wouldn't you do it? That's all I have to say at this time. Thank you, ladies and gentlemen."

SPEAKER WASHINGTON CONFERS with his aides, including Marvin Mason.

"This is the smoking gun we've been waiting for. The President just admitted he would send military aircraft into enemy territories if God told him to."

"This was just what we needed and he just gave it to us!" declares Mason.

"We have to subpoena him and make him admit this under oath, my friends," boasts Washington. "This is even easier than I could have imagined in my wildest dreams. I realize now there is a good chance I could be sworn in as Commander-in-Chief even before the election."

"We must move forward with caution." Mason advises, "We don't want to appear politically motivated."

"There is absolutely nothing for us to worry about, my dear friend," responds Washington. You can't even compare this to stealing candy from a baby. It's like the baby is simply handing me his candy."

The aides laugh as Speaker Washington continues. "Let's not waste any time. Subpoena him now, so he can answer to Congress under oath."

Twenty

THE COURT HAS reconvened. Professor Doe is once again on the witness stand. "Professor Doe, you may continue with your testimony," intones the judge. Professor Doe again removes the letter from the folder. He surveys the jury, the concerned parties, and the spectators before he begins, "Thank you, your honor. I will resume reading this document that my great grandfather wrote.

I must start from the beginning. I was born on December 12, 1787. My father, William Doe was a successful plantation owner. He was in charge of over one hundred slaves. My mother, Elizabeth, an English abolitionist, was very beautiful. Everyone who met her was in awe of both her beauty and her kindness. My father met her in Boston and fell for her at first sight. They were married a few weeks later. My father never told her until they were married that he was heir to his father's fortune, which included over fifty slaves. He knew how she felt about slavery before they were married, but hid it from her. When she learned the truth, my mother was very upset but aspired to free my father's slaves. She planned to do it through her children."

"My mother seemed to always have a smile on her face. When I got older I realized that it was because of me. I was her happiness and her hope to gain for our slaves their freedom and maybe even to help abolished slavery in our country.

One day, when I was about ten-years-old, my mother and I stood on the lawn in front of our house. Several slaves were in the yard with us, tending to their duties. There were gardeners, a boy carrying a basket of vegetables, and women washing clothes and hanging laundry. She told me, "John, when I see you, I envision a better future. I can see that the words 'All men are created equal', finally mean something. You know what I mean, don't you, John?" I responded, "Yes, mother, I do because you told me that in the eyes of God, there is no difference between us and the humble slaves."

I asked my mother, "Why does God make us white and in charge, while they are black and belong to us?" My mother replied, "We don't know the reasons why things happen. Imagine the almighty God with all the nations of this world. He chose one of them and called its people His children. Yet those children became slaves for hundreds of years until God gave them their freedom back. It will be the same with these people."

Mother also said, "God will eventually give freedom to the blacks. When that day comes, if you're still alive, my child, I want you and your children to celebrate that day with them because God will not abandon these beautiful people, just like he didn't abandon his Jewish children."

Professor Doe pauses his reading and addresses the court, "Slavery didn't end on January 1, 1863, when President Lincoln issued his Emancipation Proclamation." Slavery officially ended on December 6, 1865, the day the Thirteenth Amendment to the Constitution was ratified.

My family celebrates that day with some of our closest friends. A few of them are here right now in the courtroom, supporting us."

Professor Doe gestures toward a black couple in the audience, Mr. and Mrs. Hayes, then continues reading, "I've always told my students, including you, Mr. Black that December sixth, 1865 was the day that the worst injustice of our great country was finally made illegal. We must remember and celebrate that day. African American people should never allow their children to forget that day."

"Well said, Professor Doe." Interjects Judge Hamilton. "We will continue after lunch."

Judge Hamilton enters his chambers, picks up his phone, and calls his wife, "Emma, Please come to my courtroom to hear Professor Doe's testimony. Please take Junior out of school, so he can hear it too."

CHAPTER

Twenty-One

A DOZEN MEN and women sit around a conference table. Prime Minister Abram, of Israel, addresses members of his cabinet. "I just spoke with the leaders of China and North Korea. We're all agreed that if Fitzgerald tries to fly his so-called birds into our airspace, we will shoot them down."

Around the room, heads nod enthusiastically as the prime minister continues. "North Korea is talking about attacking South Korea now. I didn't discourage them. The Chinese are also preparing for war. Our message is clear. Our country is not at war with the United States. However, if they violate our airspace to spread that heretical message about Jesus, our religion and who we are as a Jewish nation will be in Jeopardy. The United States is a country of law. Its citizens must stop Fitzgerald."

The Israeli minister of finance raises a question. "Will you really have the American planes shot down?"

"You're damned right I will." states the prime minister emphatically. Leave it to the Yankees to try to force down everybody's throat that their God, Jesus Christ, is going to save the world. Our people need to do everything that is humanly possible to stop that. Our military is on full alert and ready. The eyes of the world are now on this Professor Doe. He's a delusional academic who lost his children and believes in a fairy tale. However the most powerful man on earth, who is about to lose his job by the way, might be willing to act on what being said on that courtroom."

Abram focuses on a rabbi seated at the table and continues. "For thousands of years, we've been serving one living God. As for that Jesus they are talking about, should I keep talking or should I stop? I'll change the subject. How will other countries react? China and North Korea will fight for pride, but us? We have so much to lose. If we are under attack, we must protect our religion. It doesn't matter who's on the other side. For our children sake! This meeting is over for now. We will meet again later today."

The prime minister then gestures to his confidant, Nahor. "Nahor, don't go. I want to speak with you."

Nahor waits for everybody to leave the room, and then asks, "What can I do?

"My job is to worry about everything– even the impossible. Call your connection." Nahor looks at him, concerned and asks, "My connection? You mean…?"

"Yes, I want Doe and his wife dead, so they won't bear any more children. Can you imagine that after this trial is over she tells the world that she is pregnant? That legend of Jesus Christ must die once and for all. We don't want our children to start believing that nonsense about Jesus. We are not going to take that chance." Upon hearing this grave request, Nahor drops into a chair, Prime Minister Abram sits down beside Nahor and advises him. "You know what you need to do. My only requirement is that the killers not be Jews."

Twenty-Two

IN THE COURTROOM, Professor Doe continues reading the letter. "I was about twelve years old when my mom witnessed and incident between me and a young slave boy who was about my age. I was hitting him and shouting that I was his master and that he shouldn't be looking at me. I kept punching him and saying, keep your head down, until my mother stopped me. She was crying and said to me. "You didn't learn anything from me. You are going to be just like your father."

We went inside the house and my dad was cleaning his gun, He looked up and noticed she was in tears. Why are you crying, what's going on? My mother wanted to talk with him in private, but still I could hear the conversation. My mother was telling my father that in the way his father had sent him to study in Boston, she wanted me to go live with her parents in Cambridge. As his only child, my father didn't want me to go and reminded my mother that he was an adult when he went to study in Boston. Women have a way of convincing men. It took me many more years to understand that. All I remember hearing from that conversation is that I was to be away only a few years and that my mother would have another baby.

A few days later, I was on my way to Massachusetts."

"Ladies and gentlemen, Court will resume tomorrow." Judge Hamilton interjects; bringing the day's proceedings to a close.

Twenty-Three

PRESIDENT FITZGERALD IS testifying before a nine-member Congressional committee, led by congressman Alan Tyson from Arizona.

"Mr. Fitzgerald, please state your name and occupation." Begins the congressman.

"My name is George Lewis Fitzgerald, and I am the President of the United States of America."

Tyson continues, "Mr. President, do you solemnly swear to tell the truth, the whole truth and nothing but the truth, so help you God."

"I do." Answers the president.

"Mr. President, you are here today not because of any political vendetta," continues Tyson, "but because we believe that our national security and our freedom is at stake. This is due to a choice it is feared you will make to send American soldier's into harm's way with their hands tied behind their backs."

"This would be a peaceful mission." Fitzgerald answers calmly.

"Mr. President," continues Tyson, "this hearing can last two or three days, or it can be over in an instant."

"Mr. Chairman, I can almost see the question you're wanting to ask burning your lips, but sir, we don't need to drag this hearing out for days until you find your gotcha moment. Just ask it right now and I will answer candidly."

Chairman Tyson jumps to his feet, upset at the president's arrogant tone.

"Are you planning to send military planes over hostile countries to drop propaganda flyers?"

"Israel is not a hostile country," replies Fitzgerald, more calmly still.

"Disturbing flyers with a faith-based message" Tyson continues, "Is what Professor Doe suggested in that Kentucky courthouse. I must add it's already been proven that what is written in his letter is a fairy tale. Professor and his wife are old with no more children to welcome Jesus on his return to glory." President Fitzgerald shakes his head in disagreement. Congressman Tyson glances around the room.

"Or will Jesus resurrect Daniel and Chelsea Doe like he did Lazarus? Asks Tyson smugly. "Is that the miracle we'll witness, dear prophet?"

Some members of the committee smirk. Others shake their heads at Tyson's disrespect.

"Mr. Chairman," responds the president, "You are wearing glasses, but you cannot see past your nose, so how could possibly hope to see what God sees? I don't know about the resurrection of Professor Doe's children, but I do believe every single word that is in that letter. Doe is the messenger for Jesus Christ, and the message being delivered is the truth. Doe's children will be present on this earth upon the triumphant return of Christ. I don't know how that will happen, but I do know that the miracle was foretold nearly two hundred years ago. It will happen soon after the verdict is read. I happen to know what the miracle will be."

A number of committee members look incredulous as the president continues.

"I am the President of the United States. Soon I will order our planes, unarmed, to drop the glory message to inhabitants of many countries, including the so-called hostile ones you mentioned. I will do this so they will know about the miracle that Jesus will perform in order for you, the pessimists, agnostics, and atheists to believe in Him."

"You are mad!" retorts Tyson. "How could you order our military to do such a thing when you are going to be stripped of your power as Commander-in-Chief in a matter of hours? This is a national emergency! Congress will vote as soon as possible to kick you out of office."

"Be happy, everyone. We are blessed. It is a wonderful time to be alive," responds President Fitzgerald.

CHAPTER

Twenty-Four

STANDING AT HIS desk, Speaker Washington is on the phone with his secretary.

"Get me the Attorney General on the phone." He demands.

He turns to his chief of staff, Marvin Mason. "We must find a way to stop Mrs. Fitzgerald in case she plans to replace her husband once we impeach him." "You're right." Acknowledges Mason. "We must act quickly."

"It seems the jury will soon decide the verdict in Jason White's case. That stubborn Judge Hamilton refuses to postpone it for us." Reveals Washington.

"How soon can we accomplish this?" asks Mason.

"The Secretary of Defense has made it clear to me that he will take orders only from the Commander-in-Chief. So I must be sworn in to take over as soon as possible."

"Mr. Speaker, Mr. Speaker" chimes his secretary.

Washington ignores her and continues talking to Mason. "We must vote within days before that fool Fitzgerald starts World War Three. This is urgent."

"Mr. Speaker, Mr. Speaker" the secretary cries again.

"What is it?

"I've been trying to tell you that the Attorney General is on hold and insists on speaking with you."

"You are useless! Maybe I should replace you with someone that can keep up. You know how much I've been wanting to talk to him." He glances at the telephone, finds a lighted button, and picks up the line.

Speaker Washington speaks into the phone. "R.J. I was just about to call you."

"I know what you want." Asserts the attorney general. I just got off the phone with the Vice President's office. They've assured me that if congress votes to remove the President from office, Mrs. Fitzgerald will not succeed him."

"Did you speak to the Vice President?" questions Washington.

"No, I spoke with her attorney." Answer the attorney general.

"R.J., things are moving fast. I don't want any trouble, so we need to cover all the bases. I will need that in writing with her signature."

"I understand, Mr. Speaker. I will get that to you by the end of the day." Assures the attorney general. Just remember everything I'm doing for you, sir."

Washington hangs up the phone before the attorney general finishes speaking. Washington then turns back to Mason and proudly states, "We're in like Flynn."

Twenty-Five

THE TRIAL OF Jason White continues. Professor Doe is on the stand where he resumes his reading of the letter. "I'd only been in Boston for ten months when I got the news that my father wanted me back home as soon as possible because my mother had died giving birth to my sister. My father never remarried. He raised my sister and I, with plenty of help, of course. I missed my mother so much. I also felt sorry for my father because I could hear him so many nights crying for her.

But I never saw any resentment in his eyes, even toward my sister. All he showed us was love. My father passed away when I was twenty-seven years old. The year was 1814. Upon my father's death, I became the richest person in the state. At that time, if you had asked me, I would have told you that I was the richest person in the world.

Twenty-three years later I had so many slaves I could scarcely count them. I was renting them out like animals all over our states as well to as other states. I was making more money from slavery than from any other business.

Many slaves worked in the field, but a few worked in the house. I heard about the following incident from an overseer. Abraham was picking cotton in the field with other slaves. They were tired, hungry and very thirsty. Working next to him was another slave, Thomas who questioned Abraham's choice to work in the field though he had the chance to work in the house. Abraham described how I had given him the choice because of his son. Thomas questioned what would happen if I became displeased with Abraham's son, Benjamin. "I am a slave. I was born a slave. I pray that I will not die a slave," exclaimed Abraham.

They continued to pick cotton all the while checking to see that the overseers, who patrolled the fields on horses, were not watching them. Abraham continued to say, "This is my hope in life, and it helps me get up every morning. I hear my son play that beautiful music. I know that it is a Divine gift. The almighty God will not abandon us. He will deliver us and give us our freedom like he did the Jewish people. Our master don't tell us those things at church, but my son can read. He told us all this." At this point, an overseer lashed out at Abraham with his whip and advises him to shut up and work. Then the overseer realizing whom he had just hit; jumped down off of his horse and begged the Abraham's pardon, offered him some water, and pleaded with him not to mention the incident to Abraham's son. Abraham excused the offense. Thomas and the other slaves started singing an old African song. The overseers look annoyed with this, but said nothing. Thomas then suggested they all take a break, knowing that they had bargaining power, at that moment.

Later, while Abraham and his wife, Lola, were eating dinner, Abraham asked his wife if their son would be joining them that evening. Lola informed him that the master's family had left on a trip that very morning, and took Benjamin with them.

Abraham then confided to his wife that when they would be free people, they would take the surname 'Hayes' and that there son would become a doctor. Doctor Benjamin Hayes.

Professor Doe then sets down the letter and drinks from a glass of water. His friend, Dr. Ben Hayes, rises, looking stunned.

"You see, Ben?" says Doe; "Our families have been friends for generations."

Dr. Hayes nods in understanding as Professor Doe picks up the letter and continues reading. "My friend, Jim Black, was in charge of the books. He was very good at head counts and keeping track of where everybody was. I owned more slaves than any other individual in the South.

I remember like it was yesterday, the day my life changed. My family and I were gathered around the dinner table, eating a wonderful dinner. I was drinking wine. My wife Jane, our son Jesse, and our daughter Carmen were all there as was our teenaged slave, Benjamin, who was entertaining us by playing music and singing. He was a young genius, about sixteen years old. We treated him and his family very well. He was almost like family to us. He traveled with us. He was even educated. My family was very pleased with this charming boy. Carmen grabbed a small cookie and stuck it in Benjamin's mouth. He smiled at her, ate the cookie, and continued playing. While he was playing, I saw my daughter wink at him. For a moment he forgot who he was. He winked back. I couldn't believe my eyes. I became enraged. I jumped up, grabbed him, and pulled him out of his chair. I yanked him toward the door. I grabbed him and told him that I was going to beat him to death. I pulled Benjamin out the front door and onto the veranda. Once outside, it felt like I was beating him for hours. My daughter ran to find Jim Black, that he might stop me from killing young Benjamin. Suddenly, I saw an angel of God standing next to Benjamin. I was standing before an angel of God. I fell on my knees. He looked at me. I could hear his voice in my head. He asked if I remembered my mother and if I remembered what she wanted me to do. He told me she was watching me at that moment. He asked if I thought she was proud or disappointed at what I'd become. Then he vanished from sight.

I keeled over and then realized that I could no longer see. I was completely blind, scared, and shivering. My wife and Jim helped me to my feet. Desperately, I screamed, "Did you see him? Did you see the Angel of God? Did you see him?" They told me they had not but that they had seen a bright light shining down from the sky like they never seen before. I asked after Benjamin. And directed them to find help for him before I passed out.

I was blind for one week. Every single hour that I was awake, I prayed and asked God for forgiveness. I promised him that if he gave me my sight back, I would do his work for the rest of my life. I would make him proud. If only he'd give me one more chance. One day I was praying and I could feel His presence in the room. "Peace be with you, John Doe, we have heard your prayers. You were chosen since the day Adam and Eve ate of the apple."

Somehow, I found the courage to speak "God, I am at your service. I kneeled down in front of him.

"I am Jesus Christ," He said, the only son of the living God. Rejoice. God will soon make this world witness a miracle, so that people may know that I am the messiah. I will show the world, especially the children of Abraham that I am the way, the truth and the life. No one comes to the Father but through me.

On that day, birds will fly and let fall my message from the sky. They will fly over China, North Korea, the nation of Israel and many other countries. Also on that day, Heaven and earth will rejoice for once they witness this divine miracle, millions will accept me as their savior.

I am also making you a promise, John Doe, when the time comes for me to return, your children will be there to witness that day. You, John, will not go to sleep with your fathers until you've witnessed freedom for the black people. Your son will be a soldier and will fight on the side of justice."

I asked when this miracle would happen.

Jesus said, "Hundreds, thousands, millions of years is but a day to the Almighty, but I can tell you that one of your descendants and one of your friend Jim's descendants will be on opposing sides of a trial. Once the verdict is read, it will be the time. You will write a letter to your first-born child, explaining this. This letter will be passed to the first born of each generation until the miracle is performed. The letter should not be shared with other members of the family. It is for the eyes of the messenger only, until the chosen time."

Once he disappeared, I opened my eyes and I had my vision back. I called my family and all the slaves on my property. I stood on the veranda, my family by my side, and the black people gathered in the yard.

"Our almighty Savior Jesus is great", I said, "and the time is near when there will be no more slavery in this country. All men will be free to go and do what they please, as it should be. For now, as long as you are on my land, you are free like any white men in this country. You are no longer my slaves, you are welcome to stay and work if you chose to, and I will pay you, like I would pay a white man. But if you decide to go, I will also help you go to different states were slavery is illegal."

The slaves cheered, and joyful shouts rose into the air as I continued. In this way, I went from being the individual who'd owned the most slaves to the individual that freed the most. I even bought more slaves, just so I could grant them their freedom. It wasn't easy. I prayed to the almighty God and he answered my prayers. I couldn't do it alone, so my dear friend Jim Black helped me. When I told him my plan, all he said was, If it's God's will, it shall be done.

We opened businesses in states where slavery was illegal. We convinced business owners into giving employment to the freed slaves I would send their way. Those businessmen were against slavery, so they were more than happy to help. God was with me because I didn't encounter rejection. One day I told my friend, Jim about what had happened to me and about the message that Jesus Christ left for my descendants to deliver. I told him that his descendants, too, would need to help reveal this message to the world and he agreed to leave instructions for his children. He acknowledged that from what he'd witnessed in the last years, he knew that God was with me.

I, John Doe, am proud to say that with Jesus on my side, I've helped thousands of slaves gain their freedom. Years before the first shot was fired in South Carolina on April 12, 1861. I was in Washington, D.C. on December 6, 1865, the day the Thirteenth Amendment to the Constitution was ratified. Therefore, I want you, my children, to celebrate this day with the black people because God gave them their freedom as promised and it was a great day for our country. Always remember December 6, 1865.

Professor Doe puts down the letter and casts his gaze at Ethan. "You see, Mr. Black, now you know and the world knows about the letter and what will soon happen.

Professor Doe continues. "Regarding your client, what is the question you wished to ask me?"

Ethan takes a minute to recover from what he has just heard then finally, he stands and begins, "Your daughter had a knife. Wasn't Jason right in defending himself?"

"Yes, but he was much stronger than my daughter. He could have stopped her without killing her," answered the professor.

"Members of the jury, all I hear is "yes", anything more is conjecture."

"Objection" shouts prosecutor Carson.

"Overruled" Judge Hamilton responds.

"The defense rests, your honor." concludes Ethan.

Twenty-Six

NEWSCASTER TOM WILSON delivers the news. "We're watching President Fitzgerald run from the White House. We now know where he is headed. He is on his way to meet with Professor Samuel Doe at the University where Doe teaches law. The President will also give a live address to the world. I say again 'the world' and not 'the nation' because his message will be broadcast around the globe. We are going to take you inside that Kentucky courtroom right now while the jury delivers the verdict."

In the courtroom, Judge Hamilton presides over the final deliberations. The jury foreman stands.

Judge Hamilton addresses him. "Foreman of the jury, have you reached a verdict?" "Yes, your honor, we have," responds the foreman.

"Jason White, please rise," instructs Judge Hamilton. He then turns to the jury foreman and requests, "Please read the verdict"

The jury foreman begins, "We, the jury, find the defendant, Jason White 'not guilty' of the crime of murder, a felony, upon Chelsea Doe, a human being."

Onlookers jeer and shout their disapproval at the verdict.

Judge Hamilton demands, "Quiet please. Regardless of how you feel about the verdict, express it outside my courtroom. Ladies and gentlemen of the jury, I thank you very much for your service. You are now free to go back home to your families. Mr. White, you are also now free to go. Case closed!"

Twenty-Seven

SPEAKER GLEN WASHINGTON is having lunch with Congressmen from his party. His chief of staff, Marvin Mason, approaches and whispers in his ear, "The Secretary of Defense wants to talk to you right now, in his office. He says it's very important."

The assistant to the Secretary of Defense ushers the Speaker into Secretary Charles Williams' office.

"Thank you for coming," Secretary William says. "I didn't want to give you this message over the phone. I wanted to let you know personally that the president gave the order and I lent my okay. Unarmed planes are leaving Alaska right now to drop flyers over Asian countries, including China and North Korea."

"He did it," acknowledges Speaker Washington.

"Yes. Other planes will be leaving soon for Europe and the Middle East." Secretary Williams continues, "We also have Russia, Israel and Iran on our itinerary."

Speaker Washington interjects, "Are you telling me that our country is at war and you haven't told me until now?"

"Our country is a country of law," responds Secretary Williams. "We have one Commander-in-Chief at a time, so until you're sworn in, I can only take order from him. If you're sworn in earlier than expected, I will have time to order our planes back before they reach China or North Korea."

"You may still have a chance to redeem yourself in my eyes, unlike Fitzgerald." Speaker Washington advises. "He will be under arrest once I'm sworn in."

"The President paid for those flyers with personal funds." Williams offers. "That's one of the reasons we didn't know about it sooner."

"What is the message on those flyers?" asks Washington. No, I don't care. There's no time for that. Raise the Homeland Security Advisory System level to 'Severe'. Keep it there until I'm sworn in."

Speaker Washington strides out of the office. In the hallway, he speaks to Marvin Mason. "Marvin, let the media know that Fitzgerald will be under arrest for treason once I'm sworn in. There will be no time for a vote. Members of Congress will only have to stand up, so I can be sworn in as soon as possible."

Twenty-Eight

THE PRIME MINISTER of Israel is meeting with his confidant, Nahor.

"The Doe's must die" he shouts to Nahor.

"Our man is already in place at the university." Nahor assures the P.M. "He will do it there, so he can make a quick getaway."

"Good," says Abram. "American planes are already in the air, but the speaker will be sworn in within minutes. So there will be time to order those planes back. The message the Christians will spread is more disturbing than I imagined. The Doe's must die so we can prove the letter is a lie. If his wife becomes pregnant, our religion as we know it will be in jeopardy."

CHAPTER

Twenty-Nine

TOM WILSON SITS at his desk. Behind him are large photographs of President Fitzgerald and Speaker Washington that include their names.

"We've just received news that President Fitzgerald will be arrested for treason," begins Tom. "This will happen once the speaker is sworn in as our new president. We expect this to take place within the next thirty to forty-five minutes. Wait. We've just received a disturbing video from inside Mr. and Mrs. Howard White's home from our correspondent, Sean. If you have children watching, we advise they not see this.

The network plays the video. In it, Sean sits near Mr. and Mrs. White, who are seated on their sofa. Mr. White puts his arm around his wife's shoulder.

Sean speaks first. "Thank you for accepting our request for this interview."

"We don't want people to think that we're evil," responds Howard White. "We're just a loving family that only wants our country to be great again."

Mrs. white nods her approval. Suddenly Jason White stumbles into the room, holding a bottle of whiskey. He's visibly intoxicated.

"Jason, do you want to join us in this interview?"

"Everyone is calling me Judas," stammers Jason. "And you know what? They're right! I could have stopped her without taking her life. I wanted to do it because I have so much hate in my heart. That's from to you, Dad. You didn't teach me anything but hate. I realize now that at a certain age, we're supposed to make our own decisions, make our own choices. So I am going to make mine right now."

Jason notices the briefcase Ethan Black gave to his father that day in court.

"Is this the money that sleazy attorney of mine gave you?" Jason demands.

He grabs the case and opens it toward the fireplace, dumping the money into the flames as his father attempts to stop him. Jason pulls out a gun.

"The money must be burned," shouts Jason. "You all know how Judas ends up, he continues. "This is for you, dad."

Jason puts the gun to his head and pulls the trigger.

IN CITIES WORLD-WIDE, throngs of people watch the televised coverage of an unprecedented event. On their screens, the image is split in two. On one side, President Fitzgerald approaches a podium. On the other, Speaker Washington prepares to be sworn in as the new President of the United States.

Member of Congress are standing up to declare their agreement that President Fitzgerald shall be impeached and stand accused of treason against the United States.

In the main gymnasium of the Kentucky university where Professor Doe teaches, President Fitzgerald holds court with his supporters. He stands on a platform, while the audience listens intently. A camera crew captures his every word.

"I know that you are all anxious about the miracle that Professor Doe said would happen after the verdict was read." Fitzgerald begins. "It's already underway. Our military birds are flying, unarmed, to deliver the following message. Rejoice. Today is the day that I, Jesus Christ, the only son of the almighty God will stand in front of the door of death. I will not let anything alive on this earth and under the sea enter, but one.

Many of you have witnessed the death of Jason White today. His death shall be the only exception. No one else on Earth will die today."

In Washington, The Chief Justice of the Supreme Court gestures for Speaker Washington to approach him.

In Kentucky, President Fitzgerald continues. "Jesus calls you all 'sons of Thomas'. Like your father, you need to see the holes in his hands and feet in order to believe. And so you shall. Today both heaven and earth are rejoicing because never in history will so many people accept Him as their savior in a single day."

The assassin hired by Israeli's Prime Minister wanders among the spectators, looking for Professor Doe and his wife.

"I wish to tell another story now," continues Fitzgerald. "There was a good family who were always ready to help those in need. When disaster struck our good neighbors in Haiti, that family was there to help the Haitian people. While there, the son fell in love with a girl. He gave her a family bracelet, telling her to keep it as a reminder of his love."

Fitzgerald looks at professor and Mrs. Doe, who stand nearby, then goes on speaking. "His sister teased him and said that their love was merely a teenage crush, but he didn't see it that way. He told his sister that this girl was the love of his life."

The killer spots the Doe's and moves closer.

"Unfortunately they lost contact with each other and the young man joined the army," continued Fitzgerald. "His military duty included a stay in Spain. That's when, by a strange twist of fate, he saw his long lost love again.

He didn't want to lose her again, so they were married then and there."

The killer fingers his gun as Fitzgerald continues the story. "The pastor that performed the ceremony called my pastor and sent me a beautiful photo of the newlywed couple.

Given my resources, I was easily able to locate the bride. I found Daniel Doe's wife with his twins, a boy and a girl."

In D.C., the Chief Justice holds up a bible for Speaker Washington to use for the swearing in.

President Fitzgerald extends his arm into the crowd and indicates Simone, Daniel Doe's wife. Those surrounding her move away, making her more visible. She's a beautiful young lady, and is holding her infant twins. As professor and Paula Doe begin walking toward her, the assassin fires a shot at Mrs. Doe. Miraculously, the bullet somehow falls at her feet. Mrs. Doe doesn't even react. The killer fires another shot, this time at Professor Doe's head. Like the first, the bullet falls at the professor's feet. The Doe's continue walking toward Simone. The crowd is absolutely stunned and amazed at the miracle they've just witnessed. The assassin is equally stunned. He begins to run for the exit, but is soon apprehended by Secret Service agents who take his weapon, throw him to the ground and handcuff him.

In D.C. Speaker Washington begins taking his oath. "I do solemnly swear that I will faithfully execute the office of the President of the United States…"

Soon, spectators begin shouting, "Stop! Stop! Miracles are happening! God is with president Fitzgerald!"

The Chinese and North Korean leaders both appear on televisions. They were about to make statements but look like they've just seen ghosts. People watch on huge screens as the image of the Chinese and North Korean leaders together.

The Chinese leader finally speaks. "The angel of God came to us and told that it is written in the book of life that the birds will fly over our countries." He smiles benevolently. And continues, "President Fitzgerald, China welcomes your birds, and we ask permission to fly alongside you."

"As does North Korea" adds the North Korean leader.

President Fitzgerald quickly responds, "Permission granted, gentlemen, and welcome!"

A South Korean reporter appears in the news coverage and in his astonishment reveals, "A few hours ago, behind me stood a fifty story building. Now all we see is debris and rubble. This building was hit in multiple missiles strikes from the North, as hundreds were working inside.

I'm told that the building also contained a daycare center for the employees, where young children were playing or sleeping."

The reporter stops to compose himself and clear his throat.

He then continues, "Miraculously, not a person is harmed! No one who was in the building that is now a pile of rubble behind me requires medical attention. This is simply unbelievable!

Earlier, government officials didn't want us to release the footage. It appears the building was hit minutes, or even seconds after the jury delivered the verdict in the Jason White trial in the United States. All those that were inside the building are giving us the same answer; that they remember nothing. They seem to have just awoken in a heap of rubble, unharmed and with no knowledge of how they ended up there.

People across the globe, as they watch these international events, drop to their knees in prayer, thanking God and giving glory to Jesus Christ.

Hundreds of Jewish teenagers from a military school are also watching these events unfolding on a large television screen. They look absolutely stunned, as if they cannot believe what they have just witnessed. Some have tears rolling down their faces.

One teenage boy approaches his commander and asks him, "Is Jesus the Messiah? Is he the son of God?"

To this the commander can only respond, "Yes, yes, he is, son. Jesus Christ is the Messiah, the only son of the living God."

They all fall to their knees with the Holy Spirit upon them.

Someone says, "For God so loved the world that he gave his only begotten son, that who so ever believeth in him should not perish, but have everlasting life." Just as in the book of the prophet Daniel.

A hand appears on the screen and in ink on parchment, writes in Hebrew, 'ליחתמ הז'. A young Jewish boy reads and whispers the translation, "It begins."

ABOUT THE AUTHOR

Daniel Jean-Louis was born in Port-au-Prince, Haiti and immigrated to the United States in winter of 1984. He is very proud to have worked as a mail carrier for the United States Postal Service. In addition to being an author, he's also a playwright, an inventor, a business owner and entrepreneur, and an ordained minister. Daniel firmly believes in a better tomorrow and that we should never regret our past but learn from our past mistakes. At this stage in his life, Daniel's goals is to be a messenger for Christ and to support and further the work of the Jeffcdomondfoundation.org founded for his late nephew, who was killed in an auto accident in 2004. Daniel is the proud father of two beautiful children. He lives in Southern California.